CW00841536

The Adventures of
Maximus Mouse

The Adventures of Maximus Mouse

Maximus and the lettuce thieves
Maximus goes on holiday
Maximus has a bad day
Maximus and the television

Brian Ogden

Illustrated by Elke Counsell

Scripture Union

Other Maximus books
Maximus Mouse
Maximus Rides Again
Maximus and the Great Expedition
Maximus and the Computer Mouse
Tales of Young Maximus Mouse
Maximus Mouse and Friends

First published as combined edition 2000

Scripture Union, 207–209 Queensway, Bletchley, Milton Keynes, MK2 2EB, England.

ISBN 1 85999 449 0

British Library Cataloguing-in-Publication Data.
A catalogue record of this book is available from the British Library.

Designed by Tony Cantale Graphics

Cover design for this edition: David Lund

Printed in Singapore by Tien Wah Press

Contents

Introduction

Maximus Mouse lives in St Michael's Church. Over the years he has had many adventures. These have usually included his best friend Patrick, Patrick's wife Paula and their forty-three children. The church and the churchyard are home to other animals as well. Barnabas the bat looks after the church when Maximus is fast asleep. Herbert the hedgehog and Robert the rabbit live in the churchyard and Johann Sebastian, the organist's cat, pops in from time to time.

Maximus got his name because to me, and to thousands of children, he is a very special mouse – a Maxi-Mouse. Maximus' adventures have been widely used in school assemblies, Family Services and read to and by children at home. In this book you can see Maximus in his true colours! These stories have previously been published as individual books.

Maximus and I would especially like to thank Elke Counsell for the enor-mouse contribution she has made through her brilliant illustrations.

We do hope that you will enjoy these adventures and find, as Maximus says in *Maximus has a bad day*, "that it certainly makes you think."

Brian Ogden and Maximus Mouse

Maximus
and the lettuce thieves

St. Michael's
Church
Morning Song

It was another fine day. The sun shone through the vestry window of St Michael's church and the birds sang, greeting the morning. The small furry creature lying under a paper hanky duvet stretched its legs, yawned loudly and began to sing.

Maximus was proud of his garden. It was near the pile of rubbish where all the flowers from the church were thrown after they had died. It had taken a long time and a lot of hard work to dig enough of the ground to plant his seeds. His lettuces were growing well.

Thinking about them, he changed his tune and began to hum the hymn that humans sing about them, 'Let us with a gladsome mind'.

Maximus struggled into a pair of grubby blue jeans which seemed to have shrunk and set off through the church. Outside the Sunday School cupboard was a pair of muddy green wellies. They belonged to Patrick who lived in the cupboard with Paula and their children. Maximus decided that Patrick wouldn't mind if he borrowed the wellies whilst he did his digging.

THE MOUSEHOLE
Patrick and Family

Just outside the church door was the entrance to one of the many burrows which had been dug by Robert and his family of rabbits. Leaning against the entrance was Robert's bright shining spade. Maximus thought that Robert wouldn't mind if he borrowed it whilst he did his digging.

When he turned the corner of the rubbish dump, he could see that Herbert the hedgehog had left his wheelbarrow after he had emptied out his dustbin onto the dump. I'm quite sure that Herbert wouldn't mind if I borrowed his wheelbarrow, thought Maximus.

As Maximus came nearer to his little plot of land, brushing past the dewy grass, he saw his lettuces, or rather where they had been. Now all that was left of the fine row of plants was a few battered stalks with all the leaves gone. Maximus could not believe his eyes and rubbed them with his front paws. There was no mistake – someone had eaten all the leaves. There was not one full leaf left on a single lettuce.

Maximus crept nearer in case the robber was still about. He looked around but there was nobody to be seen. There were no signs of paw prints anywhere – all he could see was a white slimy trail leading off towards the rubbish heap. Slowly and carefully he followed the trail which led higher and higher up the rubbish, past some very ancient chrysanthemums, and on to a prickly rose stalk. There at the top was a large, fat, black, and very slimy, slug.

'Yes?' growled the slug, whose name was Slugger. 'What do you want? Can't you see I'm sunbathing?'

'Well,' said Maximus, rather surprised and out of breath. 'You stole my lettuces. I mean they've all gone and I followed your trail up here and you did it, you stole them!' Maximus heard a noise behind him and turned round. There creeping up towards him were four more enormous slugs.

'Boys,' said Slugger to the others, 'I don't think you've met the nice Mr Maximus who grows those delicious lettuces for us. Let's say thank you to the kind mouse who looks after poor slugs who have nothing to eat. I'm sorry we borrowed your lettuces without asking!'

The slugs sniggered nastily. Maximus was stuck, surrounded by five teasing black slugs. Help arrived in the shape of a blackbird which landed close by and looked hungrily at the slugs. The slugs slid off the stalks very quickly and Maximus headed angrily back to his vegetable garden.

'They never asked if they could have any of my lettuces – they've eaten them all!' he said out loud. 'They only had to ask and I would have given them one.'

MAXIMUS!

Just at that moment he heard voices coming towards him and was surprised to see Herbert, Patrick and Robert all looking a bit cross.

'Can we have a word with you, Maximus, please?' asked Herbert. 'There are one or two things we would like to sort out.'

'Those wouldn't be my wellies you're wearing, would they?' asked Patrick.

'And that's not my spade, is it?' asked Robert.

'Surely I've seen that barrow before!' said Herbert.

'I knew you wouldn't mind,' said Maximus in a rather worried voice. 'I know you all like to share your things.'

'We do,' they said together. 'But we do like to be asked FIRST.'

'O dear,' said Maximus. 'I seem to have heard that before, and not long ago either.'

Heavenly Father,
Thank you for all the good things you give us. Forgive us when we are selfish. Help us to share what we have with those people who need it most.
Amen.

Maximus
goes on holiday

‘Four pairs of socks, trainers, towels, T shirts, trousers, toothbrush and paste, what else should I take? Will I have enough socks – perhaps I should take another pair?’ asked Maximus.

Maximus was going on holiday and Patrick and Paula were helping him to pack his case. They had already told him he wouldn't need a week's supply of hymnburgers so these had to come out of the case before the clothes went in. Maximus was going to America to visit his cousins who had gone to live there. He had never flown before and he was getting very excited.

‘There can’t be many mice that fly to America,’ boasted Maximus. ‘I am a bit special, you know.’

‘Don’t forget a sun hat – it can get very hot in America,’ said Paula, ignoring Maximus. The hat was added to the pile of clothes waiting to go in the case. When it was full, Patrick and Maximus jumped up and down on it, whilst Paula did up the lock.

‘You’re quite sure I have everything I need?’ said Maximus. ‘It is important that I look very smart. There simply aren’t many flying mice, you know.’

As they left the church, Maximus spoke to Barnabas the bat.

'Just off to America, Barnabas. Can't hang around gossiping – must fly! I'm flying on Conker, you know.'

'Maximus – it's actually Concorde,' said Patrick.

As Maximus got into the taxi to take him to the station, Robert and his family of rabbits hopped past.

'I'm off to the Useless of A,' he said. 'Going to visit my cousin Tex.'

'Er, Maximus, it's actually the U.S. of A. Meaning United States of America,' corrected Paula.

'Well, never mind,' said Maximus. 'Bye, you two. Bet you wish you were coming with me?'

A few hours later Maximus arrived at the airport, handed over his case and went through the door into the Departure Lounge.

'That really is me,' he said to the Custom's Officer, pointing to his passport photograph. 'I know it doesn't look much like it. I'm going to America – flying you know.' It was a rather old photograph, taken when Maximus wore his hair in punk style. He sat down in a very large lounge with comfortable chairs and a television screen which told about all the flights. There were planes going everywhere it seemed.

Maximus saw that there was still over an hour to wait before the flight and wandered over to the Tiny Cook café. He looked at all the food and ordered a Big Max burger.

'I'm flying on Conker to America, you know,' he said, as he paid for his burger. 'Don't suppose you meet many famous mice like me!'

He went back to his seat and watched other planes take off and land as he ate. Two white mice came and sat next to him.

'I'm flying to America,' said Maximus. 'Get around quite a lot you know, I do.'

'That's nice,' said the lady mouse. 'And what part of America?'

'My cousin Tex lives in Mouseville, Collectacat. He works in films in Hollywood – does the stunt work for

Jerry in the Tom and Jerry cartoons. 'Spect he'll take me to Hollywood to meet all the film stars.'

At that moment there was an announcement.

'Would all passengers flying to New York on Concorde please go to Gate Six.'

Maximus' heart missed a beat.

'Bye then, have a good holiday,' said the white mice.

But as Maximus walked slowly towards the exit gate he was beginning to feel nervous about going on the plane. Would the plane take off with his weight on it? What about parachutes? Did they tell you how to use

them? What happened if the pilot didn't know the way? You could get lost up in all those clouds without any signposts.

'Excuse me, sir, but are you all right?' asked a pretty young air mousetress. 'You don't look very well.'

'I don't think I want to fly,' said Maximus. 'Mice weren't made to fly. The birds are best at it, we should leave it to them. I think I want to go home.'

‘Is this your first flight ?’ asked the air mousetress.

‘Yes,’ said Maximus.

Maximus felt a very small mouse after all his boasting about flying and going to America. He was very frightened and just wished he was at home in the vestry.

The air mousetress talked to Maximus about flying,

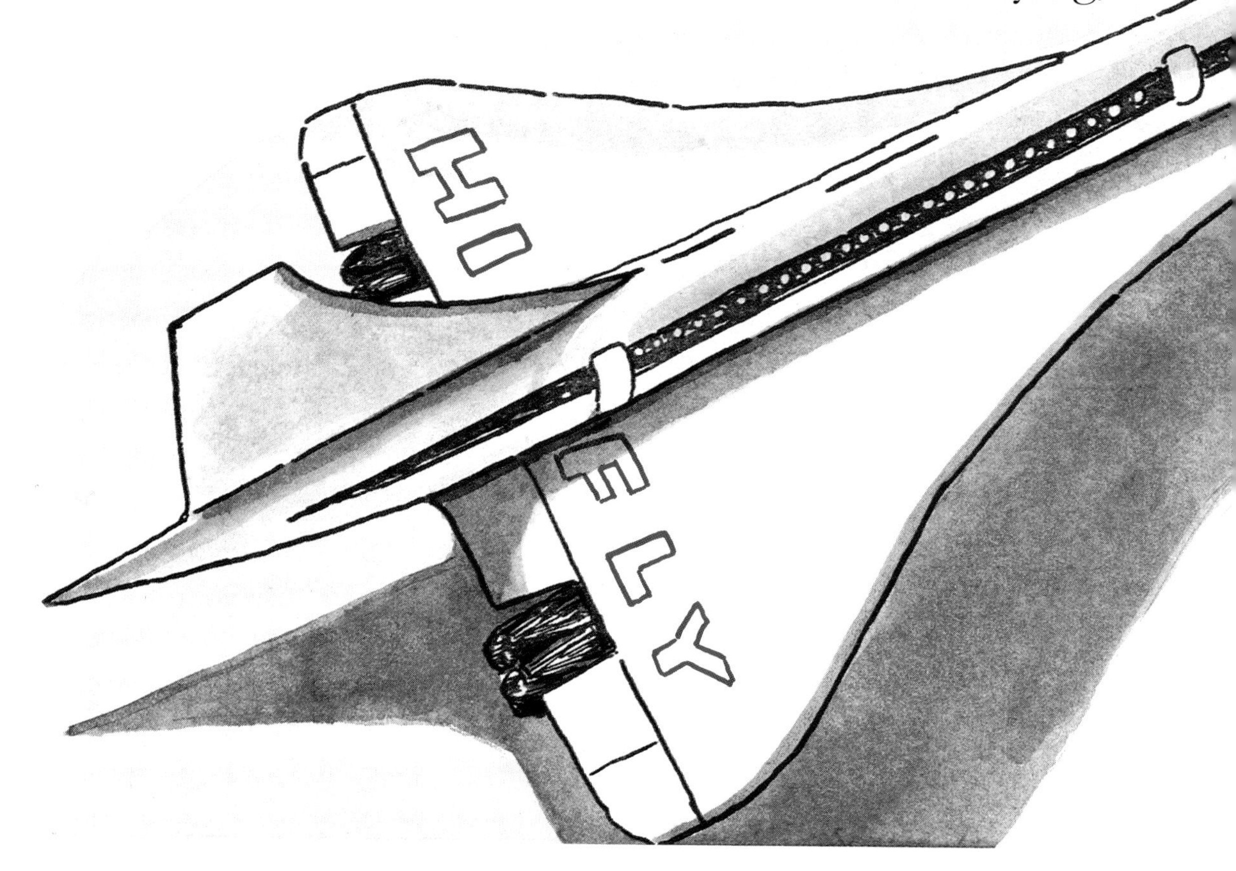

how safe it is to fly, how good the pilot was at finding his way, how everyone had a life jacket under his seat. She walked with him to the aeroplane and, at the top of the steps, introduced him to the friendly air mousetress who was on the flight.

Maximus was shown to his seat and had a wonderful view out of the window.

Maximus had a very exciting holiday in America. He visited all his cousins and in Disney World he saw the real Mickey Mouse. He went to Hollywood, met the

famous Jerry at the film studios and got his paw mark. He even enjoyed the flight back home but when

Patrick, Paula and all the children met him at the airport he thought carefully about boasting of it.

Heavenly Father,
Teach us that, whilst it is right to have pride in what we do,
it is not right to boast about it.
All our gifts come from you.
Help us to use them wisely in helping others for your sake.
Amen.

Maximus
has a bad day

'You've given me the wrong change,' said Maximus to the girl mouse on the checkout. 'I gave you a ten pound note and you've only given me change for a fiver.'

'Excuse me, sir,' she said, 'but here is the note you gave me. Look it's only five pounds.'

Maximus had been shopping and it had taken him ages to make up his mind what he wanted to buy. Should he take Whizz Pops with a plastic dinosaur in the packet or Wheaty Wonders with a water pistol? He got in another muddle over some cheese he especially wanted for a party. By the time he got to the checkout he was in a really bad mood.

'Oh, all right,' said Maximus crossly. 'I suppose I've got to believe you, but I'm sure it was a ten pound note.'

BRING FUN
INTO SHOPPING!
WHIZZ
POPS

Maximus went down the road towards the bus station and, just as he was walking over the badger crossing, the handle broke on his plastic carrier bag. His coffee jar rolled off under a parked car and his other shopping lay in an unhappy pile.

Suddenly, there was a loud hoot and Maximus leapt in the air. It was the driver of a bus who had hooted. All the passengers were laughing at him trying to collect his belongings. That wasn't the only problem. The bus that had stopped was the bus he wanted and he had to wait another half-hour for the next one.

39
39
JFEC-95

Just as he turned into the churchyard gate he saw Patrick, his friend who also lived at St Michael's, coming out of the door.

'Had a good afternoon, Maximus?' asked Patrick politely.

'No,' said Maximus.

'Sorry to hear that. What's the problem?'

'Mind your own business,' answered Maximus rudely and stamped off into the church. He took his shopping into the vestry and put it all away. As he did so, he looked again at the coffee jar – 'Bistro Gravy Browning' it said on the label. 'Oh no!' shouted Maximus. 'I can't even have a cup of coffee now.'

He flung himself on his paper handkerchief duvet and lay there in a really boiling temper. Suddenly, there was a loud bang on the vestry window. Maximus leapt off his duvet and scampered through his special hole in the wall. Just outside the window he saw a whole crowd of Patrick's children. They were playing football. It was the ball which had hit the window. Maximus marched into the middle of the group of children and picked it up.

46
4
2

'That's the last time you disturb me with this!' he shouted at them, and stormed back to the vestry carrying the ball. It was a struggle to get through the hole with the football in his paws and he knocked one knee on the bricks which did nothing to make him feel any happier.

Maximus went through the vestry into the church. As he walked down the aisle he heard a whooshing noise and felt the wind blowing in his fur. He knew at once that it was Barnabas.

'Barnabas, you beastly bat, stop it!' said Maximus angrily. 'This is no place for low flying.'

'But Maximus, I'm practising for the Bats of Britain Air Show. You know, next week when the Red Sparrows are coming.'

'Well, not here and not now! This is a church and not an airport. Leave me in peace and practise somewhere else.'

St. Michael's
Choir

Just as the bat flew out of the church, Johann Sebastian – the organist's cat – came in to fetch some music. Johann was a friendly animal and he and Maximus usually got on well. Johann was very musical and even liked Bach, after whom the organist has named him.

'What do you want?' asked Maximus crossly. 'I've just got rid of a bat and now here's a cat – I suppose it'll be a rat next!'

'I'm sorry if I disturbed you – just fetching a hymn book,' replied Johann politely. 'I shan't be long, then you can have the church to yourself again.' Maximus stamped off and soon the cat left.

'Nobody to talk to,' said Maximus to himself. 'Thought church animals were supposed to be friendly but here I am on my own again. Nobody understands that a mouse can get lonely – they all go off and leave me. Anybody would think they didn't want to see me.'

He went into the pulpit to see if there were any sermon notes to have for tea. Sermon notes were his favourite – somehow they tasted specially good. Sure enough, lying in the pulpit were several delicious-looking sheets. Maximus glanced at the top of the first one and began to read what it said. 'John chap. 15 verse 12, "Love one another, just as I love you."'

'I don't know who this John chap is but it certainly makes you think,' said Maximus to himself. 'Love each other ... er, I'm not very good at that.'

Johann
Sebastian
Barnabas
checkout
girl
Patrick

'I didn't believe the girl mouse on the checkout at the shop, I was rude to Patrick, unkind to the children with the ball, and very nasty to both Barnabas and Johann. It isn't really surprising they don't want to see me. This John chap says love one another – I really must try a lot harder.' And Maximus went off to say sorry to them all.

Heavenly Father,
We have days when everything goes wrong
and then we are unkind and hurt other people.
Forgive us when this happens and help us
to love them as you love us.
Amen.

Maximus
and the television

H. MOORE
M

'Are you coming out, Maximus? There's a Mammoth Cheese Sale at Squeaker's Supermarket today,' asked Paula.

'Sorry, but it's all my favourite cartoons on TV this afternoon – I always watch *Tom and Jerry*. Jerry's my hero. Then there's *Mouse Party* and then there's *Next Door Mice*, all about the mice in Australia. Can't possibly come out today.'

SQUEAKER'S
UNFRESH
CHEESE

Patrick and Paula went off to do their shopping, leaving Maximus propped up against the wall, eyes glued to the television.

'I don't know what we can do about Maximus,' said Patrick. 'He's worse than the children at sitting and watching TV all the time. He used to come and play footsnail or go for a long scamper over the graveyard. Now, all he does is sit and watch the box.'

'I know what you mean,' replied his wife. 'Let's see if he will come to supper this evening – you know how he likes his food. Perhaps that will get him away for a while.'

Later that evening, Patrick popped round to the vestry whilst Paula cooked a lovely meal of roast hymn book. He found Maximus in the same place as he had left him, in front of the TV.

'Sh ... quiet a moment,' said Maximus, holding a paw to his lips. 'Just want to see what happens.'

Patrick waited until the programme had finished and the advertisements started. There was one about two mice drinking a special coffee and another one with a lady mouse holding up a clean shirt, saying, 'I'll always use Percy Washing Powder – I won't swap a packet of Percy for two packets of my old powder, or for anything!'

'Maximus, Paula has sent me round to ask you to –'

'Sh ... that's my favourite ad and now I've missed it,' said Maximus. 'What do you want?'

'Maximus! Please listen for a moment. We want you to come to supper,' Patrick shouted above the noise of the TV.

'Couldn't possibly – thanks all the same. There's a special film about Blue Max – the great flying mouse. He was my great, great, great, great, great, great uncle. At least, I think that's enough greats – could be two more. Anyway, he was really famous and my mum and dad named me after him. Max, that is – not Blue.'

MAX 1

Patrick gave up and went back to Paula.

'I'm sorry, love, but I can't shift him away from the TV. He just seems to watch it all the time. He's not eating properly, he's not getting any fresh air, in fact he will make himself really ill soon. We've got to do something.'

'Well, stop worrying now. If Maximus isn't coming, then there's more food for us and the children. I think I might have a plan. I'll tell you after supper.'

At the end of the meal, Paula told Patrick what her plan was. Patrick just laughed and laughed. It was brilliant.

Next morning, Maximus had to go shopping. There were no more TV meals in the fridge, no more cornflakes in the packet, and what was most important, no food to be found by scampering around the church. It was the shops or starve.

This was the moment Patrick and Paula had been waiting for. When they were quite sure that Maximus had left the church, they hid Maximus' TV behind a curtain and dragged a large box into the vestry. They cut a square opening in the front and glued two small knobs on the side. They set the box where the TV had been and Patrick then crept out, leaving Paula behind the box.

A few moments later Maximus returned, carrying a large plastic bag full of packets of worm-flavoured crisps, cans of Mousade and a Mouse Pride loaf of bread. He settled himself down near the box and, without looking very closely, just turned one of the knobs.

Paula moved to the opening in the front of the box and began to speak: 'Welcome, viewers, to our new programme on health. Today, I am going to squeak about the dangers of television. It is a sad fact that many of you watching me will already be suffering from that dreadful disease, telisitis. Slowly, as you watch more and more television, the disease gets a hold of you. Your eyes begin to develop lines across them and the skin round the edge forms a rectangular shape. You begin to lose the use of your legs due to sitting too long. You only eat ready-made meals – I can see some of you, now, dipping your paws into another packet of crisps.'

At this, Maximus dropped the bag of crisps and started to listen even harder. Paula had great difficulty keeping a straight face and her whiskers began to twitch. She went on: 'I have come, this morning, to warn you that if you suffer from any of these symptoms then you must do three things. Firstly, you must turn off the set. Secondly, you must go outside, so your eyes get used to daylight. Thirdly, you must go for a long walk so that your legs are stretched and used.

'Now, on the count of three, follow those rules – TV off, go out and exercise. ONE, TWO, THREE.'

Maximus slowly stood up. He walked to the box and turned the knob without looking at it and went out of the vestry. By the time Patrick had crept in, Paula was laughing so hard that tears were running down her cheeks.

That evening, Maximus knocked on the Sunday School cupboard door.

'Er ... I don't suppose I could come to supper tonight?' he asked.

'Of course, Maximus,' said Paula. 'You know you're always welcome.'

'Nothing interesting on the TV tonight?' asked Patrick, nudging Paula under the table.

'No,' said Maximus. 'I choose carefully what I watch. It can get a hold on you if you're not careful! I prefer to get out in the fresh air!'

Heavenly Father,
Thank you for all the pleasure that television gives,
for what we can learn of your world and the way we can
know what is happening to our neighbours all over the world.
Help us to use it wisely and not to be tempted to sit
and watch when other things are more important.
Amen.